Introducing Lydia Monks . . .

I don't like spiders!
Why do they have to live in houses?
I think they should all live happily in the garden . . .
preferably in someone ELSE'S garden!

Why can't spiders get the message? . . .
No one LIKES them!

Lydia

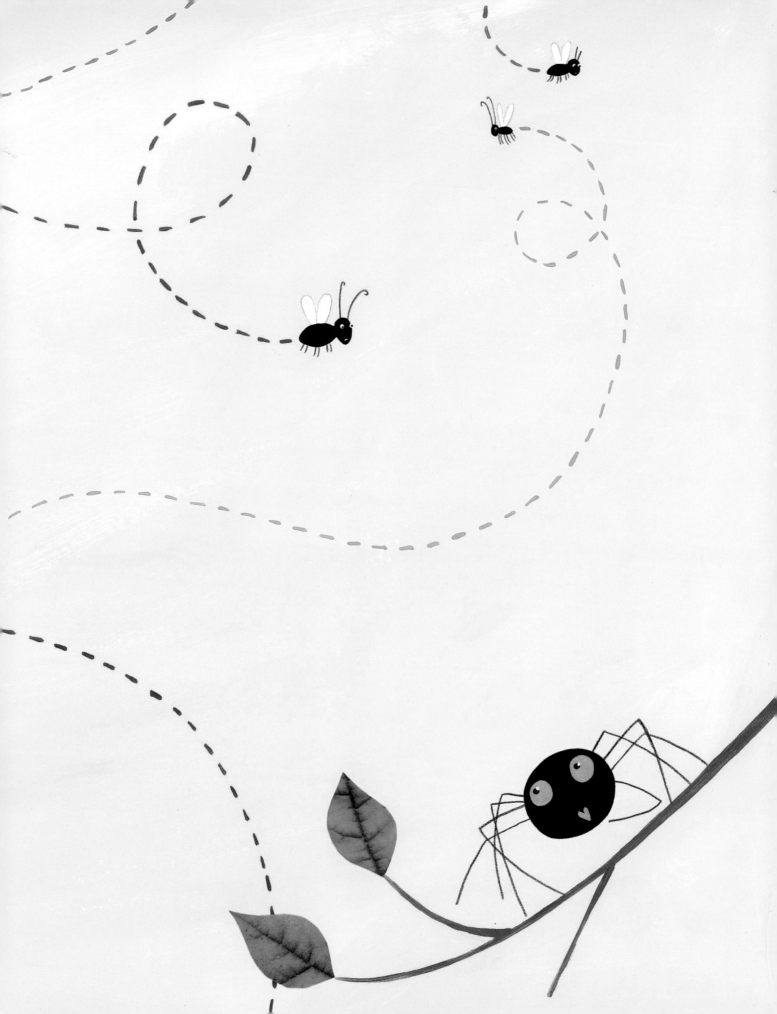

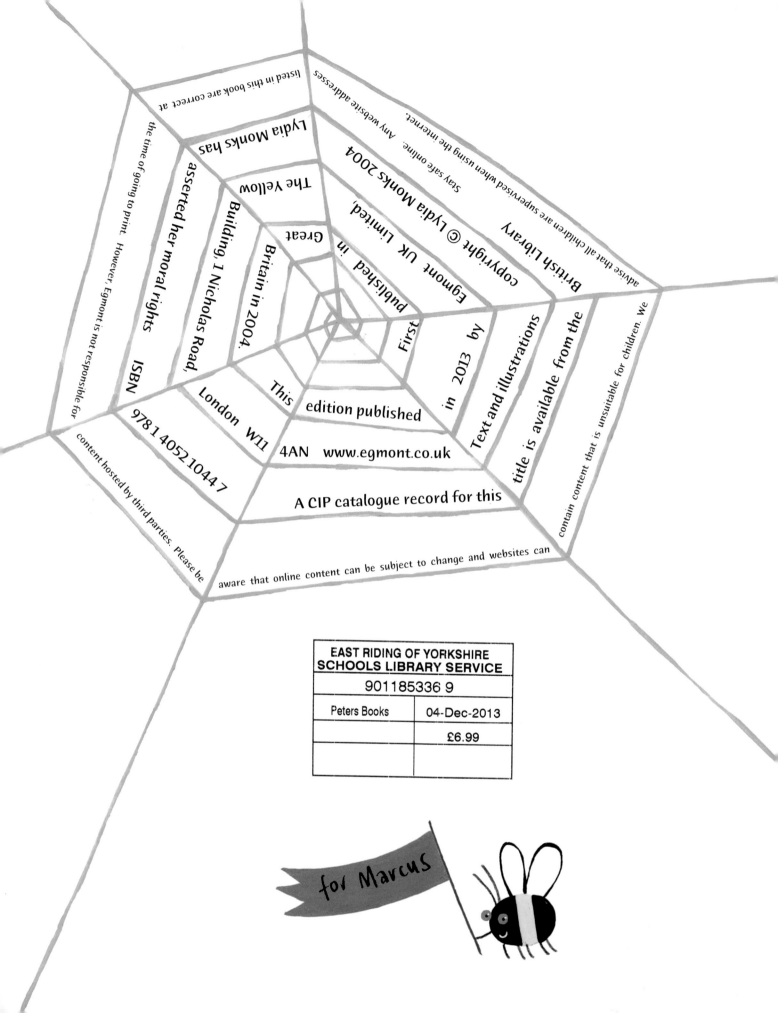

First published in Great Britain in 2004. This edition published in 2013 by Egmont UK Limited, The Yellow Building, 1 Nicholas Road, London W11 4AN   www.egmont.co.uk

Text and illustrations copyright © Lydia Monks 2004

Lydia Monks has asserted her moral rights

ISBN 978 1 4052 1044 7

A CIP catalogue record for this title is available from the British Library

for Marcus

Lydia Monks

EGMONT

It's really lonely
being a spider.
I want to be a
family pet.

THIS
family's pet!

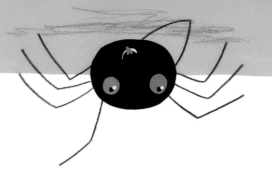

I know!
I'll show them what a great dancer I am.
None of their pets can dance like me!

"Look at me! Watch me dance!"

Oh dear!

I know!
I'll show them
how clean
I am.

None of their
pets are clean
like me!

"Out

you

go!"

Oh dear!

I know!
I'll show them how easy
I am to look after.

None of their
pets can feed
themselves
like I can!

"Out

you

go!"

It's no good.
This family will
never want me.

I'm going to go
and live all alone . . .

. . . in the garden.

I'm a real, true, proper pet!

In fact, I'm so happy with my new family,
I think I'll introduce them to all my friends . . .

More great picture books...

ISBN 978 1 4052 5423 6

Meet Babbit, a toy bunny who has
a startling adventure — that
he can't stop rabbiting on about!